"What is a man?
A man is nothing.
Without his family
He is of less importance
Than that bug
Crossing a trail."

Anonymous (Pomo), 1944

For Flying Turtle, Teacher, Coyote, and Friend.
C.R.

Copyright © 1996 by The Rourke Corporation, Inc.
Text copyright © 1996 by Gloria Dominic.
Illustrations copyright © 1996 by Charles Reasoner.

Published by Troll Communications L.L.C.

Published by arrangement with The Rourke Corporation, Inc.

First paperback edition published 1998.

Printed in the United States of America.

10 9 8 7 6 5 4 3 2

Library of Congress Cataloging-in-Publication Data

Dominic, Gloria, 1950-
    Coyote and the grasshoppers: a Pomo Legend/by Gloria Dominic; illustrated by Charles Reasoner.
    p. cm.—(Native American Lore and Legends)
    Includes bibliographical references.
    Summary: By listening to the Great Spirit and eating huge quantities of grasshoppers, Coyote
is able to save the Pomo from drought and starvation.
    ISBN 0-86593-427-4 (lib. bdg.)   ISBN 0-8167-4512-9 (pbk.)
    1. Pomo Indians—Folklore. 2. Tales—California. [1. Pomo Indians—Folklore.
2. Indians of North America—California—Folklore. 3. Folklore—California.]
I. Title. II. Series.
398.P6BD69 1996
398.2'089'975—dc20   96-5114
                                                                       CIP
                                                                       AC

Designed by Susan and Dave Albers

COYOTE
AND THE
GRASSHOPPERS

A POMO LEGEND

ADAPTED AND RETOLD
BY GLORIA DOMINIC

ILLUSTRATED
BY CHARLES REASONER

Troll

This is a story of long ago. Once, there was a sparkling lake. The Pomos who lived in the grassy hills nearby called it Clear Lake. From its crystal waters, the people fished, and no one ever went hungry. In the waters of Clear Lake, the beauty of the wide sky of the Great Spirit was reflected for all to see.

But in time, a drought fell upon the land. Little by little, the waters of Clear Lake began to dry up. The tasty fish died. The mud at the bottom of the lake turned to dust. Deep cracks, like the bare branches of trees, appeared where once the glittering water had shone.

The sun blazed day after day, and the Pomos grew hot and thirsty. Children cried for a drop of water to drink and a bite to eat. But there was no water. And there were no fish to eat. Birds and other animals became scarce. Plants withered, and there was not a berry to be found.

The Pomos gathered together. "What can we do to bring rain?" asked an elder.

A wise old woman answered him. "We must ask the medicine men."

The medicine men did all they could. They sang chants to bring water to the land, but no rain came. The people gathered and danced for rain, but still none came.

One day, Coyote was roaming the dry land. As he searched for a bit of water to drink, he heard a sound. *Bizzz-bizzz, bizzz-bizzz!*

Coyote looked up and could not believe his eyes. A large cloud was moving across the land. "What is this strange sight?" he wondered.

As the cloud moved closer, Coyote saw it was a swarming mass of grasshoppers, too many to count! The chirping of the grasshoppers filled Coyote's ears with a loud bizzing noise.

Coyote watched as the grasshoppers ate everything in their path. Each blade of grass disappeared as the insects passed over the hills. This made things even worse for the Pomos. Without the seeds from the grass, the people could not make the thick mush that was now their only food.

Coyote could not understand why these terrible things were happening. "I will ask the Great Spirit what to do," he said. "Perhaps there is a way to help the Pomos—and to get a bit of water for myself!"

Coyote threw back his head to howl. But his throat was so parched and dry, he could only make a small, rasping sound. Still, the Great Spirit answered him. "Why do you call me?" he asked.

"Times are hard for the Pomos and for all creatures," said Coyote. "Our lakes are dry. Our food is scarce. And now, to make things worse, ugly grasshoppers are eating everything in sight. We must bring water back to Clear Lake."

"I will tell you what to do," said the Great Spirit. "If you are hungry, eat your fill of grasshoppers. Then all else will follow."

Coyote did not like this advice. "Eat grasshoppers!" he said. "They do not look very tasty."

"All creatures are on earth for a reason," said the Great Spirit. "You will discover the reason for grasshoppers if you do as I say."

Reluctantly, Coyote trotted off among the insects. "I hope Great Spirit is right," he grumbled. He quickly snapped his head back and forth among the grasshoppers, catching great mouthfuls of them. Gulp, gulp! Down his throat they went.

Although the grasshoppers jumped about and tickled his throat, Coyote had to admit that they were quite filling. He continued to run over the hills, gobbling as many of the insects as he could.

Finally, Coyote couldn't eat another bite. He lay down on his back to rest. His stomach was swollen with the huge meal he'd just eaten.

Then Coyote heard a voice. It was the Great Spirit. "Why have you stopped eating? There are still many grasshoppers left."

"I am so full, there is no room for a single grasshopper!" moaned Coyote.

"Nonsense," said the Great Spirit. "Do you want to help the Pomos?"

"Yes," said Coyote.

"Then eat!" answered the Great Spirit.

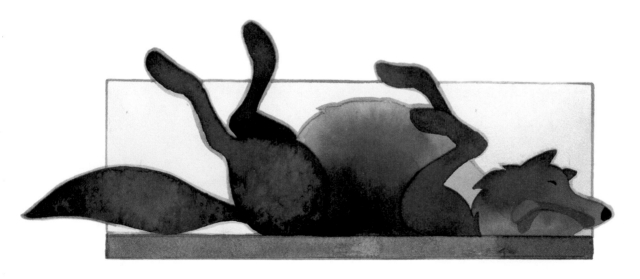

Coyote pulled himself to his feet. Again he trotted off among the grasshoppers, eating all he could. The only way he could force another down his throat was to think of the hungry Pomo children. He knew fewer grasshoppers meant there would be more grass for the Pomos' mush.

At last Coyote could eat no more. "Great Spirit," he called, "I've eaten almost all the grasshoppers. But I will burst if I eat the few that are left."

"Do not worry," said the Great Spirit. "You have done well. But I have another task for you."

Coyote yowled in disbelief. He was so full, he could hardly move. How could he possibly perform another task?

"Do you see the grasshoppers that you have not eaten?" asked the Great Spirit.

Coyote nodded.

"Follow them," said the Great Spirit.

Coyote was so full, it was hard for him to get up. Finally, he managed to sit. The last of the grasshoppers were moving in a line across the hills. With a weary moan, Coyote struggled to stand. But he could not.

Again the Great Spirit spoke. "Think of the hungry children."
Coyote did. The thought gave him the strength to stand. He set off after the grasshoppers. To his surprise, they led him straight to the patch of dry dirt that used to be Clear Lake.

Weary and still too full, Coyote was about to sink into a heap
and take a long nap. Then he heard a small sound.
Gurgle, gurgle. Coyote knew that sound. Could it be?

Yes! In the middle of the dry earth that was once a lake, Coyote
saw a tiny spring. The little bit of water made a happy sound as it
bubbled out of the ground.

Then Coyote heard a familiar voice. "Do not stop now," said
the Great Spirit. "You have work to do, if you are to help the Pomos.
Dig as deeply as you can at the spring."

"I cannot," said Coyote. "I am too full."

"Dig!" urged the Great Spirit.

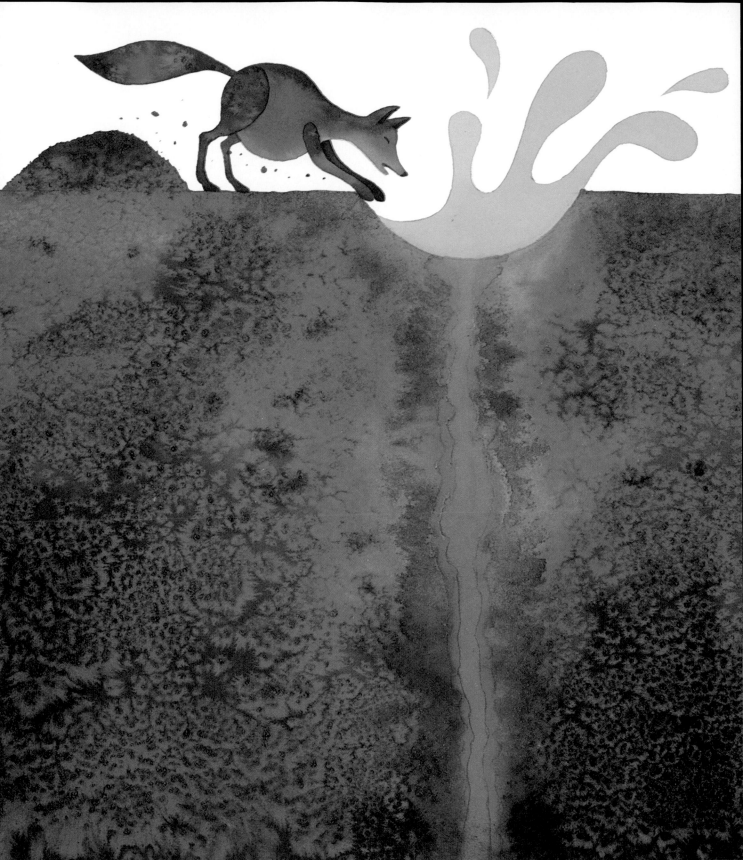

Coyote slowly dragged himself to the spring. He took a small sip. The water tasted so sweet! Then he began to dig. He dug and dug and dug. The deeper he dug, the more water came out of the ground. It ran swiftly from the hole Coyote made, rushing and swirling to fill the bed of the lake.

When at last the water stopped running, Coyote looked out upon a beautiful lake. Tired as he was, he raced to the villages of the Pomos, yowling and howling as loudly as he could.

The villagers hurried out of their huts when they heard all the noise. Coyote continued to howl. "Come see the lake," Coyote cried. "Come drink the sweet, clear water!" But the people did not understand what he was trying to tell them.

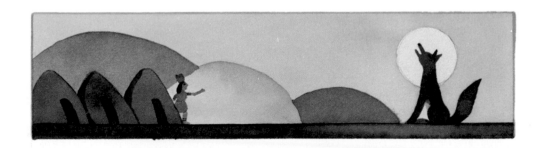

The wise men and wise women gathered. "What is the matter with Coyote?" they asked one another.

"Perhaps he has gone mad with thirst," suggested one.

"He is only begging for food," said another.

But a small child saw the fullness of Coyote's belly and knew the animal could not be hungry. He listened again to the loud howling. Then the boy thought he heard the Great Spirit whispering in his ear.

"I know why Coyote is howling," the child said. "He says the water has come back to Clear Lake."

The Pomos ran excitedly to the lake. Coyote bounded along beside them. From the top of a hill, the people stopped and stared. The little boy's words were true! The waters of Clear Lake shimmered in the sunlight.

The people drank and quenched their thirst. Coyote's heart was full of happiness at the sight. But then he heard a bizzing sound. The grasshoppers! In his excitement, Coyote had forgotten all about the few remaining insects.

Again Coyote heard the voice of the Great Spirit. "I told you that all creatures have a purpose. Now you will find out the reason for grasshoppers. Chase the last of the grasshoppers into the lake."

Coyote did as he was told. Yapping and snapping, he ran after the insects. The people watched in amazement. They had never seen Coyote act this way before.

The grasshoppers jumped nearer and nearer to the water to escape Coyote's snapping jaws. Then, bizzing and buzzing, they hopped into Clear Lake. As they did, each grasshopper became a shining silvery fish! Away the fish swam, darting through the beautiful water.

Now the people cheered. "The fish are back in Clear Lake," they cried. "We will not go hungry!"

Coyote let out one final happy howl. At last he understood the words of the Great Spirit. He also learned that a heart that is strong and unselfish can help others.

To this day, the Pomos remember the time of the drought. They tell the story of how brave Coyote brought water and bountiful fish back to Clear Lake. That is why the Pomos love Coyote!

The Pomos

OREGON

CALIFORNIA

POMO

¥

CLEAR LAKE

NEVADA

PACIFIC
OCEAN

Above. A hut made from one of the species of tule, which was too thick for finely woven baskets.

THE POMOS

Pomo Homeland

The Pomo homeland was north of San Francisco Bay, across Central California in what is now Sonoma, Mendocino, and Lake Counties. Although some lived along the Pacific Coast separated from other Pomos by giant redwood forests, most lived inland—in the sunny areas along the Russian River and around Clear Lake.

Depending on where they lived, their homes were either round or rectangular huts, covered with bark, grass, or tule. Tule is a tall reed-like plant that grows near water. These huts could house one or many related families. Villages were made up of related families with a hereditary headsman or headswoman—two if the village was large. All villages had a sweat lodge, where men met and slept. It was dug into the ground and covered with earth. Women and children slept in the huts, which were also used for cooking and storage. These homes were only for winter use. In summer, mats supported by poles or brush were enough for shelter. Big villages also had a "singing lodge," a larger structure made of earth and grass for councils and ceremonies. Families lived in the same area and harvested from the same soil generation after generation.

Pomo People

The Pomos were made up of many small groups of people who spoke seven related languages. Like other California tribes, the Pomos were hunter-gatherers. Men fished, trapped, and hunted. They also built homes, traps, and tools. Women wandered over large areas, gathering food. They also prepared food, made clothing, and raised children, who helped them gather food.

Pomos were known for their exquisite baskets. Baskets were used as traps, tools, cradles, gifts, and storage containers. They were also traded for tools, weapons, shells, and furs. Both sexes were accomplished basket weavers. They used a variety of techniques and intricate patterns. Most baskets had thirty wrappings to an inch, but Pomo baskets often had sixty or

Above. A sample of Pomo money. The Pomo men were the major manufacturers of this form of money, for their tribe as well as for many other California tribes.

Right and center. A Pomo family homeward bound with their baskets. These baskets were used to carry roots, and the spaces in the open weave allowed dirt to fall through.

more. Gift baskets were richly decorated with beads, shells, and tiny colorful feathers.

The Pomos also made money that was used by other California natives. Shells were broken into small rounded beads and strung in groups. Using these strings, Pomos were able to count into the tens of thousands. Some groups also mined a mineral called magnesite, which was baked and polished until it turned beautiful colors, like red and pink. These pieces of magnesite were very valuable and were treated like jewels.

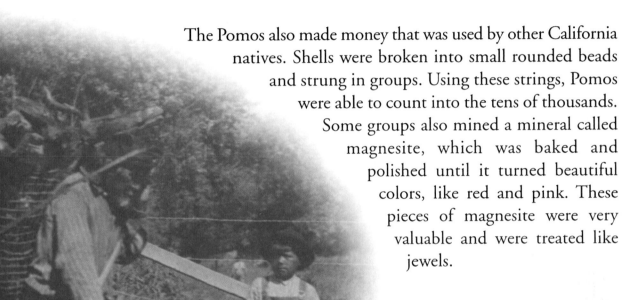

Right. One of the many ornate baskets that the Pomos are known for creating.

Food and Clothing

Men wore loincloths or no clothing in summer. Women wore skirts made of fibers from bark, grass, tule, or, occasionally, deerskin. They also sometimes wore capes that hung down to the skirts. Both went barefoot, but some groups wore skin moccasins for walking in snow. In winter, both wore furs or fiber blankets for warmth.

Food came from many sources: birds, fish, and seafood from the ocean, lakes, and rivers; berries, seeds, and roots from wild plants; small game from the forest; and acorns from the mighty oak tree. Acorns were nutritious, plentiful, and easy to store. But it took hard work before they could be eaten. Men and boys climbed trees and shook branches, or used poles to knock down acorns. Women and children gathered and shelled them. They were ground into flour by stone pestles and mortars. Water was gently poured over the flour many times to wash away the bitter acid. Then the flour was mixed with clean water. Hot rocks were dropped into the mixture to cook it into mush. Mush was eaten alone, mixed with berries, or molded into a cake and baked. Acorns were stored in large baskets in the home for one family, or in huge baskets kept above ground on poles for several families.

Top. Acorn storage caches like these were used to store acorns until the Pomos were ready to grind them into flour.

Bottom. A Pomo woman carrying her child in a tule papoose.

Top. A Pomo family dressed in their Sunday best.

Left. A multi-colored Pomo basket completely covered with shells.

39

Today, Pomo people live in cities and towns such as Ukiah and Santa Rosa, California, with non-natives, and on small rancherias instead of on large reservations.

While some have become teachers, writers, and fire fighters, many still work recreating traditional crafts and ways, such as basket making or the practice of Pomo medicine.

Top. In 1900, the upper lake Pomo people posed in front of the Frank Howe General Store.

Bottom: A basket weaver using one of the many different techniques to make a basket.

Bottom. Pomo fire dancers in 1912 dressed for a spiritual ceremony.

Top. Dancers wearing hats made with feathers.

Bottom. A boat made of tule in 1900. These boats easily became waterlogged and were brought to shore to dry out.

Right. A single tule hut.

Glossary

Acorn: The nut-like seed of oak trees

Magnesite: A light-colored mineral

Maru: A dreamer whose visions and teachings inspire religious rituals and guide the religious life of the community. Also the name of the religion

Rancherias: Areas set aside for natives to live, usually smaller than reservations

Sedge: A grass-like plant that the Pomos used for basket weaving

Sweat lodge: A structure where men meet to talk, sweat, and sleep

Tule: A tall plant with stiff stems that is only found near water

Right: A grouping of beautiful Pomo baskets. The Pomos were the experts and used a wider variety of techniques than any other tribe near them.

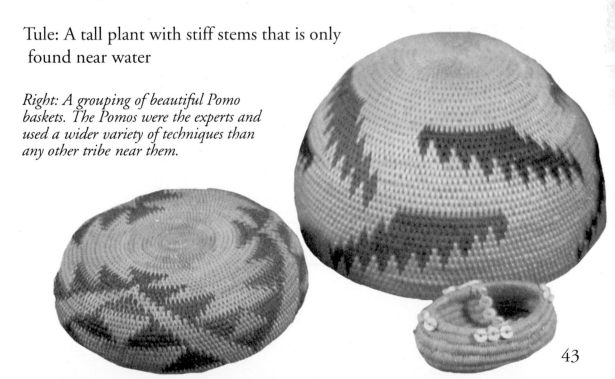

43

Important Dates

1492: Columbus lands in the Americas.

1542: Spanish explorer Juan Rodrigues Cabrillo lands along the Pacific Coast.

1741: Russian surveyor Vitus Bering surveys Bering Sea for Russia.

1812: Russian trading post, Fort Ross, established in Pomo country.

1846 - 1848: Mexican War between the United States and Mexico.

1848: The Treaty of Guadalupe Hidalgo ends the Mexican War. As part of the agreement, Mexico cedes California to the United States.

Above. A tule boat that was in the 4th of July parade for the Lake County Centennial.

1849: California Gold Rush.

1850: California becomes the thirty-first state.

1924: All Native Americans born in the U.S. declared citizens.

1968: Indian Civil Rights Act gives Native Americans the right to govern themselves on their reservations.

Above. Basket weavers, such as this Pomo woman, put many hours into making their beautiful baskets.

Top left and bottom right. Baskets displaying some of the different patterns and colors used by the Pomos.

PHOTO CREDITS

We want to extend a special thank you to Cindy Drummond, from the Lake County Museum, Lakeport, CA, for all of her help in acquiring images for this book.

Pages 32-33: Water, Photo by Dave Albers
Pomo woman gathering tule, Courtesy of the Lake County Museum, Lakeport, CA

Pages 34-35: Map by Dave Albers
Tule hut, Courtesy of the Lake County Museum, Lakeport, CA

Pages 36-37: Shell money and basket, Photos by Cindy Drummond
Pomos carrying baskets, Courtesy of the Lake County Museum, Lakeport, CA

Pages 38-39: Acorn storage cache, Courtesy of the Lake County Museum, Lakeport, CA
Pomo women and their children, Courtesy of the Lake County Museum, Lakeport, CA
Basket, Photo by Cindy Drummond

Pages 40-41: All images Courtesy of the Lake County Museum, Lakeport, CA

Pages 42-43: Dancers, tule boat, and tule hut Courtesy of the Lake County Museum, Lakeport, CA
Baskets, Photos by Cindy Drummond

Pages 44-45: Baskets, Photos by Cindy Drummond
Parade float and basket weaver, Courtesy of the Lake County Museum, Lakeport, CA

Pages 47-48: Pomo woman, Courtesy of the Lake County Museum, Lakeport, CA
Basket, Photo by Cindy Drummond
Basket, Dover Books

POMO BIBLIOGRAPHY

Bauer, Helen. California Indian Days. Garden City, NY: Doubleday & Co., 1963.

Boule, Mary Null. Western and Northeastern Pomo Tribes. Vashon, WA: Merryant Publishing, 1992.

Brown, Vinson and Douglas Andrews. The Pomo Indians of California and Their Neighbors. Happy Camp, CA: Naturegraph Publishers, 1969.

Editors of Time-Life Books. The American Indians: The Woman's Way. Alexandria, VA: Time-Life Books, 1995.

Emanuels, George. California Indians. Walnut Creek, CA: George Emanuels dba Diablo Books, 1990.

Heizer, R.F. and M.A. Whipple. The California Indians: A Source Book. Berkeley, CA: The University of California Press, 1971.

Kroeber, A.L. Handbook of the Indians of California. New York: Dover Publications, 1976.

Maxwell, James A., Editor. America's Fascinating Indian Heritage. Pleasantville, NY: Reader's Digest Association, 1978.

Sturtevant, William C., General Editor. Handbook of North American Indians: California (Volume 8). Washington: Smithsonian Institution, 1978.

Waldman, Carl. Encyclopedia of North American Tribes. New York: Facts on File, 1988.

Worthylake, Mary M. The Pomo. Chicago: Children's Press, 1994.

Above. A Pomo from Long Valley. She is between 110 and 120 years old.

Right. A Pomo basket adorned with shells.